# A Little Singing Bird

By Lucy M. Blanchard

Illustrated by Katherine G. Healy
Cover illustration by Nadia Gorski
Cover design by Tina DeKam
First published in 1923
This unabridged version has updated grammar and spelling.
© 2019 Jenny Phillips
www.thegoodandthebeautiful.com

To
# JOHANNA HUTCHINGS SPRAGUE

IN RECOGNITION OF HER
UNFAILING INTEREST
IN MY WORK

# Table of Contents

1. THE MIRACLE ................................................................ 1
2. THE LITTLE SINGING BIRDS! ................................... 3
3. IL CANARINO—THE CANARY ................................. 5
4. LITTLE ROSA CAVELLI ............................................ 10
5. A SHREWD BARGAIN ............................................. 15
6. JOYOUS HOURS! ...................................................... 19
7. NUMBER ONE-TWENTY-FOUR ............................ 24
8. THE VISIT OF THE PRIEST! .................................... 29
9. BEPPO AND THE BIRDS ......................................... 35
10. ORO TO THE RESCUE ............................................ 41
11. PROSPERITY ............................................................. 47
12. MARCHING FEET .................................................... 50
13. THE MASCOT OF THE COMPANY ...................... 55
14. THE RED, WHITE, AND GREEN .......................... 57
15. A DREARY CHRISTMAS ........................................ 60
16. THE LITTLE GOLDEN FEATHER ......................... 65
17. THE HOMECOMING ............................................... 70
18. THE MARRIAGE FEAST ......................................... 73
19. THE KING DOES NOT FORGET ........................... 76
20. HAPPINESS ............................................................... 79

# 1

## The Miracle

*Such a little thing! Such a dainty little thing!*
*All made up of trills and tremolos:*
*And yet so brave of heart!*

The Canary Islands lie off the northwest coast of Africa. The shores are steep and rocky, and the surface is diversified with mountains. There are various forms of vegetation, from the date palm of the plains to the laurels and evergreens farther up the mountains.

Canaries are also native in other parts of the world, but it is in these islands one likes best to think of them—these islands of sweet scents and tropical fruits, of blue sky and sunny stretches, of sea breezes and of lofty mountains towering to the heavens.

Few are left in these their native haunts, for way back in the fifteenth century, we are told, some shipwrecked mariners trapped the little singing birds (wild things of joy and sunshine) and, when rescued, took them to their homes in England.

Borne thus in triumph, prisoners in the close hold of a sailing vessel, it would have been no wonder if they had died from fear.

A storm came up. The ship tossed and rolled. Great waves rose and threatened destruction. Rescued and rescuers quarreled over the course, and mutiny resulted. The cargo of canary birds was quite forgotten.

Suddenly, the clouds parted, and a ray of sunshine made its way into the hold.

And then . . . the miracle!

Above the roar of the storm and the din of angry voices came a clear, sweet note.

A sound from heaven? The sailors stopped and listened. Another note, and yet another.

At last, one of the rough fellows, awestricken, whispered hoarsely, "The birds! The little singing birds!"

And so it proved.

In the midst of peril, one of the tiny feathered prisoners, taking heart at the gleam of sunshine, was lifting up his soul in song.

Nor was that all. It was not long before he was joined by others. And while the mariners wondered, the chorus swelled in trills and tremolos.

As they listened, the rough men took heart. They ceased to quarrel among themselves and, after taking counsel together, steered the vessel into safer waters.

And thus the first canaries came to England's shores!

# 2

## THE LITTLE SINGING BIRDS!

News travels fast, even without the modern aid of telephone and telegraph, and it was not long before all of merry England knew of the wonderful cargo that had been brought from the faraway islands.

The canaries were the talk of the court and of fashionable society, while in the streets and country lanes, one would stop another to ask, "Have you seen the birds, the little singing birds?"

They were first displayed for sale in a stall of the public market, and thousands came to look at them. Many varieties had been captured and brought over, varying in color from a soft gray, which merged into green, with patches of yellow conspicuous upon their breasts, to shades more nearly golden.

To the average person, the color of the feathers meant more than the quality of tone, and one vied with another to secure those with fancy markings. But there were some who came and bought, not hastily, but only after listening to every note, and having made a careful selection, took them away with the serious intention of breeding the birds for the clear, sweet beauty of their song.

Thus came into existence a new industry, and it was soon discovered that these little feathered creatures could be trained to sing more beautifully in captivity than in their native haunts.

They became the rage in Britain, a household pet in the gilded rooms of Hampton Court and in the meanest hovel of London's poor.

The great Queen Elizabeth did not scorn to while away the hours listening to one of these dainty songsters, and who knows but that Mary Stuart, in her captivity, may have found the time less tedious because of a little singing bird?

It was not long before they were carried into distant lands and, from that time to this, have held first place in the hearts of people in almost every corner of the civilized globe.

# 3

## Il Canarino–The Canary

It is a far cry from England of the sixteenth century to the year 1913 and old Guido's aviary in Naples, Italy.

A far cry, yet the little singing birds are as much in favor at this later date as when they were first shown in the marketplace in London.

How or when they came to Italy, I cannot say; perchance some vagrants from their native isles found their way across the sea to this sunny land. But it pleases me to fancy that it might be possible to trace the descent of this bird of which I write to the little prisoner who first cheered the hearts of the despairing sailors on their rough passage.

Be that as it may, in the days before the Great War, old Guido was a breeder and trainer of canaries in Naples, Italy.

In his younger days, he had been a famous performer on the flute, and in his old age, he was never so happy as when playing to an audience of feathered songsters who showed their appreciation by making strenuous efforts to reach the high notes.

He would bob his head as he played and exclaim, from time to time, when some note sounded clear above the others:

"*Bene! Aha! Bene!*"[1] or, laying aside his instrument, almost beside himself with joy, would cry:

"*Evviva*! I am *contento!*"[2]

It was Guido's custom each morning to make a tour of the aviary, beginning with the nesting room.

On this particular occasion, his limbs trembled with eagerness as he softly opened the door a crack and thrust in his head.

This was the day, the eventful thirteenth day, when, according to canary schedule, the eggs in a certain nest should be hatching.

The walls of the room were lined with boxes, tier on tier, each box containing a nest in which a little canary hen patiently brooded over tiny blue eggs.

Before each nest stood her mate—on guard.

The old man cleared his throat. Every little female raised her head, startled at the sudden sound, and every male looked anxiously in the direction of the door. Then, reassured at sight of the familiar black skullcap, they settled quietly back into their usual attitudes.

Hark! A sound of chipping shell! Guido's practiced ears placed it at once as coming from the upper right-hand corner.

His cane almost fell from his hand, and he hobbled as fast as his rheumaticky limbs would permit to the box where his prize singer, Raffaeli, stood at attention. The bird fluttered about excitedly, anxious to communicate the all-important news, and the solicitous mother did not remonstrate when the old man, having picked some broken fragments of shells from the floor, gently caressed her dainty wings.

---

1     *Good*

2     *Cheers! I am pleased!*

He found it difficult to contain himself at the sight of two scrawny, naked little heads, with big bills pushed out from under the maternal breast.

Hark! The chipping began again. Other eggs were hatching.

"How, now, my pretty!" he exclaimed to the anxious father, stroking each dainty feather and looking affectionately into the beady eyes as he treated him to a hemp seed from his pocket. "So, you've your family at last, Raffaeli! If only one of them shall prove as fine a singer as yourself, I shall be satisfied. I wager there's no better in all Italy."

Talking thus, half to himself and half to the bird, he lingered about the cage until he had assured himself that all of the eggs were safely hatched.

Then on he passed to the other nests, inspecting each in turn.

For every little inmate, he had a special word of greeting, never failing to address each one by name. It was plain to see that a close bond of sympathy existed between the master and his feathered pets.

It was astonishing how fast Raffaeli's family grew. In the four birdlings Guido took great delight and fairly gloated over the two who early showed signs of emulating their talented father.

As soon as possible, these were transferred to the training room, to be with other promising birds, that they might not hear a single false note but receive special instruction in voice culture.

Here, they were kept in the dark—the curtains being lifted only when the master entered the room with his flute under his arm.

And such a welcome as he had—the little songsters vying

with each other in joyful greeting.

Then, one by one, they would be taken into an adjoining room and given the lesson of the day.

How Guido would play! And how rapturously each earnest pupil would burst into song, quavering and trilling until the notes sounded high above the flute!

At a single false note, he would stop. And, after severely reproving the culprit, would repeat the strain again, and yet again, until he was satisfied.

Then he would clap his hands and cry:

"*Bene! Bene!*"

Promising though they all were, the first-hatched son of Raffaeli was easily superior. Taking the attitude of an opera singer, he would trill and trill in ecstasy until the pure tones rose even above the high notes of the flute, and the master would cry:

"Aha! Aha! You excel them all! You are *Il Canarino!*"

He grew to be a handsome fellow, with breast of softest yellow, and with wings that shone almost like gold.

At last the day came when even the critical master could not but pronounce him fully trained. As he was just then sorely pressed for money with which to pay the rent, and as, moreover, he knew a certain shopkeeper, Cicho by name, who was always glad to purchase a fine canary, there was no excuse for holding him any longer.

With a heavy heart, old Guido carried him to the dingy little shop in the Piazza del Mercato, receiving in return merely enough *lire* to pay the month's rent.

Tears filled his eyes as he parted with his favorite, and all the way home he lamented, repeating to himself, "*Oime!*[3] There will never be such another voice! Ah, me! Ah, me!"

---

3   Alas!

As for *Il Canarino,* for a few moments he was greatly depressed. He missed the master and his companions. He did not like the shopkeeper's greedy eyes as he gloated over his new purchase and, with a rough hand, felt the little quivering throat, exclaiming: "Such a syrinx! Such a beast! *Bello canarino!*[4] I can sell him for double!"

He resented his surroundings. Hung high in a little cage, he looked down upon a pile of old junk, odd bits of copper, cheap imitations of Roman lamps, heads carved from lava, all lying helter-skelter.

Then, like the brave bird he was, he rose above his surroundings, threw back his head, and sang like a very Caruso.

---

4    *Pretty canary!*

# 4

## LITTLE ROSA CAVELLI

On the fourth floor of one of the oldest and shabbiest buildings, in a certain side street of Naples, lived Alessandro Cavelli, with his wife Margherita and their little daughter Rosa.

Alessandro and Margherita were natives of the lovely Isle of Capri; he, the son of a vinedresser, and she, one of the fisherfolk of the bay.

They had lived in Naples ever since their marriage. And for many years, Alessandro had worked in a macaroni factory. Their quarters were poor and cramped, and the din of the city streets, and the smell of garlic that floated in at the window, at times seemed unbearable, so it was no wonder that they often sighed for the clear air of their island home.

But to Rosa, it was an enchanted realm. She loved to stand on the balcony and watch the varicolored garments which hung on lines that stretched from one side of the street to the other. How they fluttered and billowed in the wind! By craning her neck, she could catch a glimpse of Vesuvius, with his glowing crown of fire by night and his waving cloud of smoke by day.

As for the street below, it was a never-failing source of

amusement, crowded with people, dogs, donkeys, and other animals.

She adored the heavily laden donkeys and would laugh aloud when she saw a sun-browned peasant guiding one of them by the tail, while the little red tassels dangled bewitchingly over his stubborn ears, and the tiny bells tinkled as he made his way up the street that was scarcely more than a flight of steps.

In a window opposite was a green parrot that talked incessantly and was her special delight, and there were a countless number of lean, tortoiseshell cats.

There was scarcely a moment in the whole day when a procession of some kind was not passing—there were priests in black, monks in brown, sailors in blue; there were the macaroni vendors with white, streaming lengths of pasta; there were always the cries of "*Pesce! Pesce fresche!*"[1] and "*Paga! Paga!*"[2]

Occasionally, a *tamburinaio*[3] with his pyramid of tambourines would look up and smile as he called his wares, or a *portatore di acqua*[4] would stop to flavor a glassful of water with a squeeze of lemon and hand it to some thirsty mortal.

No wonder the dirty, busy street had such a fascination for Rosa, and when the strains of "*O Dolce Napoli, O suol beato*,"[5] came floating up to her window, she would stand very still, listening in a kind of ecstasy.

Every morning she would be on the alert for the first sight

---

| 1 | *Fish! Fresh fish!* |
| 2 | *Buy!* |
| 3 | *tambourine seller* |
| 4 | *water carrier* |
| 5 | *O sweet Naples! O blessed soil!* |

of the *caprajo*[6] driving his goat. And as soon as he turned into their entrance, she would run to fetch a little cup and open the door that he might not be kept waiting. She would watch, with wide-open eyes, as he drove the goat up the narrow staircase. And when she took the foaming cup, she would lay her hand gently on its head and say, "*Grazie,*[7] good Loretta!"

She liked to watch her mother cooking in the dark little kitchen. No one else could make such good *allese,*[8] and she couldn't imagine anything nicer than a steaming platter of spaghetti.

Sometimes, on Sunday, her father would ask, "Would my little Rosa like to go to the park by the bay?" And, with a joyous glance at her mother and a happy, "*Si! Si!*"[9] she would hurry as fast as she could to put on her red shoes and the new dress with the bright sash.

Then how sedately she would walk between her father and her mother, who was always very dignified in her best striped skirt and black bodice. At least, Rosa would try to walk sedately, but, in spite of herself, the little red shoes would dance ahead.

After the band had stopped playing, they would stroll about the grounds with hundreds of other happy, carefree people, or perhaps watch the strange creatures in the aquarium—stately white fish that looked curiously at her from behind the glass; wicked, evil fish; delicate structures of coral, and dainty little things that floated about and resembled nothing so much as bits of gossamer.

---

| 6 | goatherd |
| 7 | Thank you |
| 8 | chestnut soup |
| 9 | Yes! Yes! |

Ah, those were wonderful afternoons!

Once in a very great while, they would take the boat and join the lively crowds bound for places down the bay.

Her father would stand in the bow, and as the breeze blew fresh and cool, he would bare his head and murmur: "*Il mare! Il mare!*"[10]

As for Margherita, even Rosa could see the color come into her cheeks and the new light in her eyes as she looked toward Capri and Ischia, lying like jewels in the distance.

Then, how the mandolins and guitars would tinkle with the strains of *Funiculi, Funicula, Il Trovatore,* and other loved Italian airs! Sometimes her father would give her a *centesimo*[11] to put in the cap when it was passed. And when the musician smiled, showing his white teeth, and murmuring, "*Grazie*," she would blush and run as fast as she could back to her refuge between her father and her mother.

Once, on the way to Capri, they spent a wonderful hour in the Blue Grotto, lying flat on the bottom of tiny boats and drifting through the small entrance into the fairy cave. At first, Rosa was terribly afraid—it was all so strange! Her dress that her mother had taken so many pains to make—as white as snow—was blue, as were her hands. But when she saw that her mother and father were as blue as herself and caught sight of gaily colored jellyfish, she was delighted and cried, "*Bello! Bello!*"[12]

After they reached Capri, they climbed up a long, winding road to the vineyard and the little house where Alessandro was born and where his toothless old mother still lived.

She gave them a touching welcome, and they ate their

---

10  *The sea! The sea!*

11  *a penny coin*

12  *Pretty! Pretty!*

simple luncheon of black bread and olives under a gnarled, old grapevine. And when at last they bade her goodbye, she lifted her withered hands above their heads and murmured a benediction that brought tears even to little Rosa's eyes.

They were soon on the way to the boat, pausing a moment to place a nosegay at a wayside shrine, and then on until they met some peasant women carrying upon their heads baskets of trinkets such as tourists love. And Margherita cried:

"See, little one, that is as I was when I met your father!"

"Aye," responded Alessandro, "and your hair was as black as night and your lips as red as ripe cherries. There was no one who could shake the tambourine and dance as you could."

But Rosa was plucking at his hand. "The pretty trinkets! See Papa, the red, red beads!" Nor would she be satisfied until he had purchased a strand of tiny corals and clasped it about her neck.

It was almost six o'clock when they reached Naples. The child was very tired with the long day, and her little feet lagged as they left the steamer and threaded the busy streets on their way home.

But as they turned the corner of the Piazza del Mercato, she darted suddenly ahead. Above the din of street noises, she had caught the blithe notes of a little canary.

# 5

## A Shrewd Bargain

"Mama! Papa!" she cried, seizing first her mother's hand and then her father's hand in her excitement. "The bird! The bird!"

"*Si! Bello canarino!*" echoed her mother as her eyes followed the direction Rosa indicated. "And what a voice! It's like a flute!"

By this time a crowd was closing in front of the window, and Alessandro was obliged to elbow his way through in order to get anywhere near. Even then Rosa was so short that he swung her up on his shoulder, just as Cicho, the shopkeeper, appeared in the doorway. His greedy eyes narrowed into little slits of delight as he saw the attention his newly acquired purchase was attracting.

"*Si! Si!*" he reiterated, rubbing his hands. "It is *Il Canarino!* It would be hard to find another like him. Yet"—he swept a shrewd, appraising glance through the crowd—"yet, one must live." He raised his voice. "Is there anyone who would like to own this fine bird?"

"*Si! Si!*" Rosa cried, her eyes glowing with emotion, and her lips parting as her breath came and went. "Ah, *si!* Ah, *si!*"

In her excitement, she scarcely realized that she had spoken out loud. And when the people nearby turned curious eyes upon her, she hid her head in embarrassment on her father's shoulder.

But the shopkeeper had already singled her out and addressed his remarks directly to Alessandro.

"*Venite!*[1] What will you give?"

Rosa trembled with excitement. But her father shook his head. "I have not the money with which to buy."

"*E peccato!*"[2] Cicho sighed. "I sell him very cheap, almost for nothing."

Just then the notes of the canary rang out sweeter and purer than ever, and Margherita caught his arm and whispered, "I, too, would love the little singing bird!"

Cicho saw her motioning and was quick to pursue his advantage. "To you, I will sell him very cheap. *Quaranta lire*[3] is all I ask."

Alessandro emphatically shook his head. "I have not so much in all the world, and what I have must go for food."

"*Trenta lire!*"[4]

Resolutely, Alessandro put the child down, saying shortly to his wife, "Let us go!"

"Twenty-five—even twenty, though it would ruin me!"

At Cicho's offer, Rosa's lips quivered. Would her father still refuse?

He turned, hesitated, put his hand in his pocket. "It is impossible! I have not enough!"

A big tear rolled down Rosa's cheek.

---

| | |
|---|---|
| 1 | *Come!* |
| 2 | *It is a shame!* |
| 3 | *Forty lire* |
| 4 | *Thirty lire!* |

In an instant, the shopkeeper was at his side, whispering ingratiatingly:

"Come, what have you? For you, I will make it even less!"

Alessandro jingled the bits of money in his pocket, then took out a collection of dirty paper notes, besides a few lire and a large number of copper coins. Slowly he counted them out. They amounted to fifteen in all.

Cicho's eyes were now the merest slits. It was more than he had thought. With difficulty, he restrained his joy and repeated sadly, "It will ruin me, but to you I give him!"

With that, he swept the whole into a grimy leather purse, went back to the shop, took down the little cage, and pressed it into Alessandro's hands.

"There—he is yours. Take him quickly, lest I repent!"

Overcome with delight at having thus the bird in their possession, neither Alessandro nor Margherita noticed the look of satisfaction on the shopkeeper's face. He had made a shrewd deal and had more than tripled the price he had paid old Guido.

As for Rosa, she was so overjoyed she could scarcely walk steadily, and she didn't know what to say when her father placed the cage in her arms, saying, "The little singing bird is yours!"

She wanted to laugh, and she wanted to cry. But she did neither, only murmured an ecstatic, "*Grazie!*" and put her face close to the wires of the cage and looked straight into the little beady eyes.

As for *Il Canarino*—at first he did not know what to make of it all. But there was something in the way the child held him that inspired confidence, and when her soft, black eyes looked so tenderly into his, he was satisfied.

He was *her* bird, and he, too, was happy.

He was tired after the long day, and the little swaying motion with which she carried him was very soothing. So, before he knew it, he was sound asleep, all puffed out like a ball, with his head buried in the feathers of his shoulder.

Nor did he awaken all the way home, although Rosa was so sleepy herself that she stumbled twice on the narrow stairs, and Alessandro was obliged to carry the cage the rest of the way himself.

Not until he had placed it on the table in the shaggy living room, and they had crowded around to admire and love, did the little canary open his eyes. Then, with a satisfied chirp, he was off in the land of dreams again, and he did not even waken when Alessandro hung him by the window which, henceforth, was to be *his* window.

## 6

## JOYOUS HOURS!

Rosa awoke at the peep of day. Was it really true that they had brought home a canary the night before, or was it all a dream?

She strained her eyes, but in the dim light, she could not see clearly across the room. In another moment, she was out of bed and stealing, in her little bare feet, to the window.

Holding her breath, she opened the Venetian blinds. Yes, the cage was where her father had hung it. Very quietly, she clambered up on a chair and lifted one corner of the dark handkerchief that Margherita had thrown over the top so that the little bird might not waken them early.

Perhaps, after all, he was not there! Suppose he had been spirited away during the night!

And then she saw him, his head still buried in the feathers on his shoulder.

"*Buon giorno!*"[1] she whispered, and drew back, frightened at what she had done. A quiver of the wings, a raising of the dainty head, and two little black beads of eyes looked into hers.

"I didn't—mean—to wake you up!" she faltered. And, in

---

1   Good morning!

response, the bird gave a cheery "good morning" chirp and began at once to preen his feathers.

Without another word, she guiltily made her way back to her bed in the opposite corner, but the mischief was done, and it was not many minutes before *Il Canarino* was singing lustily.

There was no more sleep for anyone that morning, and though her father and mother suspected what had happened, they did not have the heart to find fault with their little daughter.

After breakfast, at the mother's suggestion, Rosa placed the cage on the table and gave the bird his first bath in his new home.

How he enjoyed himself as he splashed to his heart's content and ruffled his dainty feathers—then carefully smoothed each one into place!

And how they admired him! Rosa watched in breathless adoration while Margherita called her attention to each special point of excellence.

"See his beak, how thick and high it is? That is so he can eat seeds easily. His body, how slender, and his throat, how it quivers and throbs as he sings. Is he not wonderful, our little canary!"

She paused a moment, then went on doubtfully, "But he must have a name. I like not *Il Canarino*. It is too long and hard to speak."

All day long she thought in vain. And when her husband came, he found her still undecided.

"Beppo! Chito! Toto! A dozen names have come to me, but there is not one of them I like."

For some moments Alessandro stood before the cage without comment. The last rays of the setting sun touched every feather with glory. How golden the breast! How radiant the wings!

"*Si!*" he cried. "I have it! He is *l'Oro*, the golden one!"

"It is true," Margherita said, greatly pleased. "He is gold, pure gold!" While Rosa softly clapped her hands and echoed, "Oro!"

It was surprising what a difference a little singing bird made in the home. It seemed as if he were fairly bubbling over with contagious happiness the livelong day.

Needless to say, he had everything in his cage that he could possibly wish—a nice piece of cuttlebone on which to sharpen his bill and the best seeds that could be bought for him. There was always a crisp leaf of lettuce or a bit of apple tucked in between the wires. He quickly learned to take hemp seed from Rosa's fingers. And the swing, which Alessandro took so many pains to adjust, was his special delight.

As time went on, he became somewhat of a tyrant. When Alessandro suspended a tiny chime of bells in his cage, he discovered its possibilities at once. If the shutters were not opened and the dark handkerchief removed as early as he wished in the morning, he would impatiently ring the little bells. Especially on Sunday mornings or holidays, when they would have liked an extra wink or two, the peremptory "Tinkle! Tinkle!" would force the family up against their wills.

He knew Alessandro's steps on the stairs, and the moment he opened the door would call an ecstatic greeting.

After a few days, Margherita ventured to take him out of his cage. At first he seemed frightened, but when she gently stroked his feathers and held him close, that his wings might not flutter, he gained confidence and snuggled down in the palm of her hand as if he enjoyed its warmth.

Soon she let him fly, and presto! Away he went, straight to the clock-shelf. She had placed a broken bit of looking glass to attract him, and it was not long before he discovered it and, like Narcissus, became enamored with his own image.

Coquettishly he cocked his head, first on one side and then on the other, uttering joyful chirps. Then, like the vain little fellow he was, he preened his feathers and struck charming attitudes all his own.

When Rosa approached him, he showed plainly that he didn't wish to return to his cage but ran along the top of the clock-shelf, looking back saucily from time to time. Then, much to their amusement, he let down his tail, as a brake, and slid along on the improvised rollercoaster.

Having thus tasted the delights of freedom, he was no longer content unless he was allowed to fly about the room at least once every day. He would utter little pleading cries. And if no one came at once to his help, he would work his beak about the fastening of the cage door until he succeeded in prying it open. Then out he would fly, and he often surprised them by lighting on their shoulders or pecking at their fingers.

He loved to try experiments with his voice and had a trick of throwing it so that it seemed to come from an entirely different direction.

At times they would search vainly for him in the kitchen, only to find him standing close beside them on the window ledge. He learned to whistle and to warble, although he was at his best when he reached the flute-like notes old Guido had taught him.

So the days passed. Sometimes, inspired by his joyous song, Margherita would feel herself a girl again and would get out her tambourine, wind a bright sash about her waist, and dance the Tarantella. She would seize little Rosa, crying, "Let us dance!" Then, guiding her footsteps, together they would whirl and twist and bend as she shook her tambourine, while Oro nearly split his throat in a frenzy of joy.

So Alessandro would find them on his return from work. And, in his worn workman's blouse, with his red kerchief about his neck, he would join them, forgetting the fatigue and worries of the day in the mad, graceful figures of the dance.

# 7

## NUMBER ONE-TWENTY-FOUR

An exhibition of any kind is an event to the Neapolitan, so when Alessandro brought home the news that a bird show would be held the next *festa*[1] day, there was great excitement in the little family.

"We will go, and Rosa with us," Margherita exulted. "She shall see them all—the fine hens, with the roosters and the downy little chickens, the magpies and nightingales, besides the green parakeets, and—" She stopped as an idea came suddenly to her mind, an idea that made her catch her breath at the very audacity of it.

"Alessandro!" she cried. "Alessandro! What say you to entering our Oro?"

He looked at her in amazement. "What a woman you are to think of such a thing!"

"Why not?" she pursued. "We know no bird can sing as well, and if he should chance to win a prize, it would indeed be a great honor!"

"*E vero!*"[2] he answered reflectively. "Why not?" And yet, to one who, heretofore, had been only a humble onlooker on

---

1     party
2     That is true!

such occasions, the thought was quite startling.

As he paused doubtfully, Oro, who had been unconcernedly flying about the room, alighted on the clock-shelf and began singing cheerily, as if in approval of the plan.

"Oro—hear Oro sing!" put in Rosa. "He wants to go. Please, let us take him to the show!"

So it was decided, and a few days later, Alessandro came home through the Via Roma, at the farther end of which was the exhibition hall. He felt awkward in his workman's blouse as he approached the glib-looking man in charge but felt relieved at finding the requirements so simple.

"Bring the bird in the cage any time before nine tomorrow morning. He'll be entered at once. There'll be a hundred or more like him, I presume."

Alessandro's heart sank at the careless words.

"A hundred more like him!" Would there not be danger of his being lost in so great a number?

"Don't worry!" the man continued kindly, divining his thought. "We give you a check for identification purposes."

So that was how they did it. He breathed a sigh of relief but still waited, uneasily shifting from one foot to another, and finally faltered, "I—don't quite—understand—about the awards?"

And again the attendant helped him out.

"The judges make the decisions. You'll find a card tacked up on the wall on the day of the exhibition, giving the points to be noted. There are red, white, and blue ribbons. The blue means first honors and is only given to the best singer. Can your bird sing?"

"*Si! Si!*" Alessandro responded eagerly.

The man laughed. "So everyone thinks. All birds are wonderful to their owners! I would advise you to take your chances but not expect too much."

With that, he waved his hand for the next comer, and Alessandro moved slowly away.

His confidence shaken, his footsteps lagged as he made his way homeward and wearily climbed the stairs. Suppose they should be disappointed. It would go hard with the wife and the little Rosa.

Would it not be best to persuade them to give up the idea? He reached that point in his reflections just as he was turning the knob of the door.

Suddenly, a clear note of greeting rang out, and then another, still higher.

His confidence returned. There were not many that could sing so well.

Thus reassured, he patted his little daughter's arm and addressed many jocular remarks to the bird himself.

"Tomorrow—ah, tomorrow will be the great day when you will have a chance to show what you can do. Be sure you win the blue ribbon. Neither the red nor the white will answer!"

In reply, Oro sang one of his most cheerful airs, and Margherita danced about the room with her arm around Rosa's waist, crying:

"*Si! Si!* It will be a great day for us when Oro comes home with the blue ribbon!"

Nevertheless, there was little sound sleep for anyone that night. Rosa tossed uneasily in her narrow bed, and twice Margherita roused her husband to ask if he thought the bird's voice was in good condition.

The next morning, they were up very early. Even Oro seemed to understand that it was a momentous occasion, for he took what seemed like an interminable time to enjoy his bath and smooth each separate feather.

At last he was ready, and they set out, Rosa insisting on carrying the bird, although the streets were crowded and noisy. From time to time, she stopped to whisper endearing words in his ear, and her own courage kept up wonderfully until they reached the hall and the clerk at the door held out his hand for the cage.

Then a great sob shook her little frame. She buried her face in her mother's skirt and wailed, "I can't let him go! I can't! I can't!"

"But it must be!" Alessandro's voice was firm as he took the cage from her and passed it in, receiving in return a dirty piece of cardboard with the number "124." Then on they pushed, there being no time to linger, for the hallway was crowded with people bearing pets of all kinds to be placed on exhibition.

On entering the hall, they found a perfect Babel—roosters crowing, hens cackling, and chickens peeping from the corner set apart for their special benefit. There were parrots talking, doves cooing, and magpies chattering. As she looked around, Rosa dried her eyes. It was interesting, especially the great owl who stood solemnly blinking on his perch above her head.

Over one door was a hand and a sign which read, "This way to the canaries," and Rosa's heart beat faster as she kept a tight hold of her father's hand and passed into a large room with a temporary scaffolding erected in the center. There, on different tiers, were placed the cages. There must have been at least one hundred and fifty. Over each cage was a dark cloth, for no canary was allowed to use his voice until he had been tried before the judges. Each cage was numbered, and anxiously they looked for 124. At last they found it. The middle cage on the upper tier.

Poor little Oro! There was nothing he disliked so much as to have a dark cloth over his cage. Rosa could imagine just how he was standing on his perch, puffed up disconsolately.

They stood there for a few moments, idly speculating as to the inmates of the other cages, until Alessandro noticed a card tacked up on the wall giving the points to be considered. He read it aloud with some difficulty:

"1. General appearance.
2. Position of bird when singing.
3. Quality of tone."

He puzzled so long over the second point that a kindly attendant undertook to explain it to him.

"You see, some birds stand awkwardly on their perches and exert themselves too much. Again, they open their bills too wide, and that isn't pleasing. All these things count with the judges."

Margherita's heart sank. The hand that held little Rosa's trembled, and the child looked up anxiously.

"Does Oro open his bill too wide?"

"I—don't—know!" Her voice broke a little.

It might even be. Not one of them had ever noticed how wide he opened his bill when he sang.

"And why should a bird not open his bill wide when he sings?" her husband asked indignantly.

Then, noting her evident distress, he put his arm half around her and added, "But do not worry. The main thing is the tone, and in that our canary must surpass them all. Did not the shopkeeper himself call him *Il Canarino*?"

Somewhat comforted, she brightened up, although she could not quite dismiss her anxiety. And all the way home, she kept repeating to herself, "*Oime!* It may even be that he opens his beak too wide when he sings!"

# 8

## THE VISIT OF THE PRIEST!

As for Oro, it was no wonder that he felt puzzled as to what it was all about. It wasn't that he minded being carried through the streets. Though the noise and din were a trifle disturbing, Rosa's little hand on his cage and her words of love and endearment were reassuring.

"We're going to a bird show," she whispered once, bending over. "And you must look your prettiest and sing your best because, you see, we want you to win the prize."

And again, when she heard a dejected little chirp, she held the cage up with an encouraging: "It's only a little way longer, my Oro!"

On the steps of the outer hall, she paused to say, "We have to leave you here, you know, but you mustn't be lonely, because we'll take you home tomorrow."

Her own courage had held out wonderfully. It was only when the moment came to surrender him that she had broken down and her father was obliged to take matters into his own hands.

From that time on, the little canary was in the depths of despair. He didn't like the way he was swung along by the careless attendant, and he simply hated being kept in the darkness.

His mistress had told him to "Look his prettiest and sing his best," but how could he do either with a horrid cover over his cage? No wonder he lost heart and moped on his perch as every one of his one hundred and forty-nine miserable companions did!

He did not rouse when he was taken into an adjoining room and placed on a table, around which sat three spectacled, dignified judges. And he was too discouraged to care, even when the covering was taken from his cage.

He caught some of the conversation which was being carried on in a low tone, but it was about "general appearance" and "position," two things which he neither understood nor had any interest in. In fact, he conceived a positive dislike for the round eyes that peered appraisingly at him through the bars of the cage.

Then, suddenly, his courage came back, and, like the cheery little fellow he was, he rose above his surroundings and sang his very best.

"*Bene! Bravo!*" burst from the lips of the spectacled men. "*Bello canarino!* Sing again, my golden one!"

Encouraged by their praise, he began again, whistling, warbling, trilling, rolling.

They were quite beside themselves, these staid judges who were prepared to weigh every point carefully. After all, what did points count?

He was easily superior to the others in quality of tone, and they were wildly enthusiastic, exclaiming over and over again, "How he took the high notes! And without the least exertion! He is *the* bird."

With one accord, Oro was awarded the bit of blue ribbon, carried back in triumph, and placed on the platform in the middle of the upper tier.

Utterly unconscious that he had been so honored, he unconcernedly watched the crowd who surged about him, calling him the "prize singer" and uttering endearing epithets.

Little did he care for their admiration! In his canary mind, he was probably speculating how long it would be before his little mistress would come to take him home.

As a matter of fact, she and her mother and father were already making their way, as best they could, through the surging, betting crowd to the room where the canaries were.

There are no people in the world that give the impression of being as utterly carefree and lighthearted as do the Neapolitans. They sing and play and dance with seeming utter abandon. And yet, a fear is always present in their minds.

Over the volcano ever hovers a waving cloud of smoke by day, a glowing torch by night. Almost without warning, the forces of nature may break their bounds, and destructive fires may belch forth from the crater.

Even in the midst of his merrymaking, the Neapolitan, from time to time, glances uneasily in the direction of the great mountain. Perchance he turns a cartwheel to the delight of surrounding urchins; as he straightens up, he gives an instinctive glance to assure himself that Mt. Vesuvius is all right. It is his last thought at night and the first in the morning. A darkening of the sky, a rumble beneath the earth's surface, is enough to cause anxiety.

And so it happened that, on this particular afternoon, when the rooms were crowded with laughing, happy throngs of men and women, accompanied by innumerable children, the gathering of black clouds in the direction of the mountain, a noise like artillery, a slight earthquake, brought a feeling of terror to every heart.

Within the past months, there had been insignificant manifestations, slight explosions of lava and ashes, rumbling that had been heard for miles, and then subsidence, resulting in nothing more serious than slight changes in the crater's rim. Yet, there was always the thought that next time might prove destructive to home and life, and with this thought came panic.

Blacker grew the sky, louder the rumbling, and the birds cowered in their cages. The restless crowing of cocks, the excited cackling of hens, the terrified chatter of the magpies, the mournful hoot of the owl, added to the weirdness.

In the general stampede, there was danger of people being crushed to death. Some fell upon their knees, praying for the protection of the Almighty. The authorities were powerless to stay the panic. The old priest lifted his hands in a vain effort to calm the surging mass of people.

The sun was still some hours from setting, and the bright rays falling through the western windows contrasted strangely with the darkness from the opposite direction.

Suddenly, the notes of a little canary were heard, high and clear, above the noise of the surging, terror-stricken crowd.

A miracle?

No, only a little singing bird. People stopped and listened. There was something in the song that inspired courage. Instinctively, they became quieter, and men stooped to lift the sobbing children in their arms and carry them to safety; women moved more slowly; the birds ceased their terrified screaming.

In another moment, the other canaries, following his example, were singing lustily. The earth's rumbling ceased, the dark clouds over the volcano's head were dissipated—

Vesuvius was quiet, with only a new gash on the crater's edge.

The exhibition rooms were quickly emptied as the people, cheerful and smiling, bore away with them their pets. On every side, laughter was renewed, for the good Lord had been with them.

All tears and smiles, Rosa, with her father and mother, at last reached the room where the canaries were still singing. In an instant, her bright eyes caught sight of the bit of blue tucked in the cage, and she could scarcely wait to get it in her arms. Then, with tears of joy falling through the wires, she uttered little crooning cries:

"And you are safe, my Oro! Safe with your bright eyes and your yellow breast! It was like you to sing so bravely when everyone else was frightened to death! *Ē vero*, you won the blue ribbon! I knew all the time you would."

She bent her head closer and caught a satisfied chirp as the bird realized it was his beloved mistress talking.

But that was not all—the authorities did not forget the incident, and a few days later, the old priest climbed the steps of the shabby building and called upon the Cavelli family.

Margherita herself answered the knock, her knees trembling as she saw the revered man on the threshold of their humble home.

"Nay, woman, do not fear!" he spoke reassuringly. "I bring with me a little recognition from the city for the service rendered by your brave bird. The authorities appreciate that it was owing to his song that the panic was averted."

With that, he pressed into her hand a purse containing five gold pieces and a tiny cross marked: "For the bird whose song was the means of saving many lives."

Scarce knowing what she did, Margherita mechanically took it from his hand, then knelt while the good priest murmured a benediction on the house.

A moment more and he was gone, and but for the cross and purse, she would have thought she had been dreaming.

"*Venite!*" she cried, calling Rosa to her side, "come and see what the good priest has brought. The cross we will sew to the bit of ribbon, but the gold pieces we will keep for your marriage portion!"

So saying, she carefully hid the purse in the back of the old clock.

When Alessandro came home that night, he would have thought her full of vain imaginings, and would have doubted her story, had she not opened the door of the clock and counted out the gold pieces while Rosa showed him the tiny gold cross sewed to the bit of blue ribbon.

Silently his hands sought the beads of his rosary. Then, with a voice trembling with emotion, he looked up at the little canary who was swinging happily in his cage and exclaimed, "The cross and the gold pieces are, indeed, wonderful. But more than all else is the blessing you have brought to the home, our golden one!"

# 9

## BEPPO AND THE BIRDS

The news spread. For days people came from far and near to see the bird who had become famous. Most of them had canaries of their own, canaries who sang all day long and delighted their owners' hearts, but not one of them had ever won a prize.

And to them all Margherita showed the blue ribbon and told of the visit of the good priest, even allowing them to touch, with reverent feeling, the tiny cross. But not one word did she say of the gold pieces hidden in the back of the clock.

"One never knows," she sagely cautioned Rosa. "One never knows. They're all honest enough; it isn't that I doubt them, but times are hard, and there are some who might be tempted—and never again would the Virgin send gold pieces for your marriage portion."

At night, after relating the incidents of the day to her husband, she would take out the little purse and, like a miser, count over the coins to assure herself that they were all there.

As for Oro, it would have been a wonder if his dainty head had not been a trifle turned at the praise lavished upon him; and if he gazed longer than usual in the bit of looking-glass, surely no one could blame him.

He became more than ever identified with the family interests, with each passing day singing himself farther and farther into their hearts and lives.

When Alessandro came home at night, weary with the day's work, it was Oro who sounded the first joyous welcome.

When Margherita wilted in the warm summer days and was sick with longing for the sea breezes of her island home, it was the little bird that made her forget her languor and brought again the color to her cheeks.

When Rosa fell downstairs and broke her ankle, it was he who helped the long, dull hours to pass and, when at last she walked, rejoiced with her in blithe chirps.

When, toward fall, a dark-eyed *bambino*[1] came to the home, Oro nearly burst his throat in rapture, and it was his song that cheered Margherita in her days of weakness.

As the *bambino* (Beppo, they called him) grew and thrived, the first thing his baby eyes noticed was the canary flying about the room. With his first conscious effort, he stretched out his arms to the fluttering thing that perched on the side of his crib, and the first syllable lisped by his baby lips was "Or'! Or'!"

When they placed the cage on the kitchen table for his daily bath, Margherita would gently turn Beppo's head so that he might see the canary splashing in the water, and would say, "See how he loves the bath, even as you must, little one!"

One night Alessandro came home with a new and larger cage, in which he proceeded to install Oro, whispering all the while soothing words in the puzzled ears.

"There have been times, my golden one, when you have been lonely. Alessandro guessed it. And since the old

---

[1] baby

quarters are small and cramped, he has brought you this new cage, that you may make a home of it and be *contento* with a dear companion."

And so it came about that, when he put a fluttering little lady in the door, Oro chirped a blithesome welcome and flew to meet her. She was a modest little thing, not so bright in color as *Il Canarino*, and was clearly frightened as she gently repulsed him and crouched, trembling, in one corner close to the slender bars.

"*Benissimo!*" exclaimed Margherita. "Let us call her Pippa and pray that they may be happy together!"

As for Oro, it was plain to see that she took his fancy at once. And after casting admiring glances in her direction, he set to work to make himself as attractive as possible, laying each golden feather in place with studious care and puffing out his breast until it looked softer and fluffier than ever.

Then he sang—oh, how he sang! Pleading notes, soft and sweet, until, in spite of herself, she turned her head to listen.

Instantly, he edged a trifle nearer. His tones became more passionate as he trilled and warbled and whistled in an effort to tell her how happy he was that she had come to share his home and be a dear companion.

Was it any wonder Pippa's heart was won? What little canary could resist such ardent overtures?

Soon they were beside each other on one of the perches, uttering soft love notes.

When, at times, she would herself venture timidly to ruffle his feathers with her bill, one could see he was beside himself with joy.

After a few days, the door was left open, and they were given the freedom of the rooms. Then how happy Oro was! And how eager to show her all his favorite places! Together, they slid along the clock-shelf, and her head was reflected beside his in the bit of looking-glass. He led the way to the crib, and there they perched, touching bills, until Beppo held out his hand and cooed with glee, while Rosa clapped her hands in sheer delight.

Meantime, Margherita fastened a little framework of a nest to one of the wires and left some bits of cotton carelessly about, every shred of which was discovered by the happy pair and proudly smoothed into the softest linings.

At last, one morning, Margherita, finding Pippa patiently brooding on the nest, with Oro standing jealously on guard beside her, gently lifted the dainty wings and disclosed four tiny blue eggs.

Pippa was a conscientious little wife and brooded, motionless, for hours while Oro watched beside her, like the faithful husband he was.

When she wearied or needed exercise, he was always ready to take her place while she swung lazily back and forth or flew about the room.

It was Rosa who discovered that the eggs had hatched and heralded the glad news.

"Mama! Mama!" she cried. "Come, see, there are three baby birds! I saw their heads pushing out from Pippa's wings!"

Margherita left her baking in the kitchen, and Alessandro was late in reaching the macaroni factory that morning because he stopped to lift the dark-eyed Beppo so that he, too, might see the little birds.

"They are Pippa's babies!" he exclaimed. "And what a proud father Oro is, to be sure! Now he will have plenty to do to keep the hungry mouths fed!"

Rosa was so excited that she forgot all about the milk, and

the *caprajo* had to thump hard on the door before he could make himself heard. Then nothing would do but he, too, must see the new birds. And while they were all engrossed, the goat himself walked unconcernedly into the bedroom and chewed up Rosa's Sunday shoes before anyone noticed he was there. But that was a mere incident, and he was allowed to go unpunished.

Ah, that was the reddest of red-letter days. And when Alessandro came home that night, Rosa ran half down the stairs to tell him that Oro never left his cage all day, he was so busy feeding the new babies, and that she had named them Koto, Chita, and Pip.

"And, Papa," she cried, "Koto is the largest, Chita has the brightest eyes, and Pip, why, Pip, he is the smartest of all!"

It was not long before the little birds learned to feed themselves, their feathers grew, and the awkward forms became more shapely and graceful. Then began the lessons in flying, in which both father and mother took part, coaxing them from perch to perch until they dared venture on longer flights in the outside world.

So Rosa found them: Pip, triumphant beside his father on the clock-shelf; Koto, fluttering his wings in the door of the cage; while Chita lay helplessly sprawling on the floor with her anxious mother hovering over her.

One morning there was an unwonted air of excitement about the cage, and it was plain something unusual was on the docket. Oro chirped so peremptorily to his little wife that Margherita, for a moment, feared lest a family quarrel was pending. But when Pippa and Chita flew out of the door, leaving possession of the cage to the masculine members of the family, she guessed that Oro had decided it was time to try their voices.

So it proved, as was plain, when Oro took his position on the perch in the center of the cage and chirped to Pip and Koto to range themselves opposite.

This done, the lessons began. Oro would give quick little chirps and stop until Pip and Koto answered him. If the particular tone they struck suited him, well and good. But if not, his beady eyes would flash fire as he uttered a little scolding cry which evidently meant:

"Try again!"

And try they would—again and again, until the stern teacher was satisfied.

Every morning the singing lessons were resumed, becoming more difficult as time went on. Soon it was evident that the pupils were entering more and more into the spirit of it. All unconsciously, they would emulate their father's very attitude as well as do their best to reach the desired tones.

Of all this time, Margherita and Rosa were most interested spectators and would listen eagerly as the birds trilled, whistled, rolled and warbled.

"*Bene! Bene!*" they would cry. And when, from time to time, they held up little Beppo so that he, too, might see the pretty sight, his baby coos would mingle with the birds' chorus.

## 10

## Oro to the Rescue

Then winter came—such a winter as seldom comes to sunny Italy. It was cold and damp, the clouds hung heavy over the head of Vesuvius, and the sun refused to shine for days at a time.

One afternoon Alessandro came home chilled to the bone, and the next day he was racked with fever. Margherita, distracted, hung over him as little Beppo, neglected, wailed piteously, and Rosa, frightened, shrank into a corner of the room.

Days passed and Alessandro was no better. The doctor shook his head and prescribed medicine, warmth, and good nourishing food.

Alessandro's wages had never been large, and now that he was laid aside, the little savings rapidly diminished. Fuel was scarce and high, and since the sun refused its warmth, the fire of a few sticks of charcoal made little impression in the large, high-ceilinged room, with its cold stone floor.

After some weeks the outlook was still more discouraging; the sick man was losing steadily. It had taken the last of the little fund to pay the rent, and Margherita was well-nigh distracted as to how she could buy more medicine and fuel, to say nothing of the good food which was now more than ever necessary.

Margherita herself had had almost nothing to eat for three days, and the children would have been hungry, indeed, had it not been for the *pasta* sent in pity from the macaroni factory, and for the good *caprajo,* who still climbed the stairs and bade the goat fill the little cup with milk, although he had not been paid a *centesimo* for at least a week. For the first time, Alessandro had refused to eat the chestnut soup which Margherita had prepared to tempt his appetite.

What should she do? It was late at night, and for hours she sat at her husband's bedside, listening to his labored breathing and trying to solve her problems. Suddenly she rose resolutely and, going to the clock-shelf, exclaimed:

"There is no other way! We must use the gold pieces brought by the priest!"

She felt like a thief as, after a glance at the children asleep in the corner, she stealthily took out the purse and counted over the coins.

They were all there. Speculating on how long she could make them last, she took one and tied it in the corner of the handkerchief. When they were gone—but her mind refused to consider further. She crossed herself before the print of the Virgin that hung above the clock, murmuring, "Forgive me for using what was sent for the little Rosa's marriage portion!"

She had carefully placed the handkerchief under her pillow when she remembered she had not said goodnight to the birds, something she never failed to do.

Crossing the room, she lifted the covering from the cage and softly whispered, "*Buonanotte!*"[1]

---

1   Good night!

In response, Oro raised his head with the drowsiest of drowsy twitters. And, vaguely comforted, she herself went to bed.

All through the night she lay there, thinking. But not to sleep. That drowsy twitter had suggested another solution to the problem. Putting her hand under the pillow, she felt for the knot in the handkerchief. Perhaps, after all, it might not be necessary to use Rosa's money. For an hour or two, she lay. Rising, she groped her way to the shelf and replaced the gold piece in the purse.

Oro had come to the rescue!

A clock on one of the towers was striking the hour of five. The first dawn was beginning to break in the east. It was not too early to dress, if her plan was to be carried out before the children awoke.

Soon, with her shawl on, ready for the street, she stood before the cage of canaries. Then she faltered. Pippa's babies! How she loved them, every one, and yet it was absurd to keep them all, and she knew well that it would not be difficult to sell them. She could take one this week and the others later, if necessary. Her spirits rose. Who knew but that her husband would soon be well?

Then came the difficulty of deciding which one she should choose. They were darlings, every one of them, and never had they looked so attractive as in the early dawn.

Rosa's heart would be broken if her favorite Pip were missing in the morning; he was such a delight with his smart tricks. No, she would not take Pip. And Chita—Chita was the comfort of her mother's heart; she would leave her. Well then, it must be Koto, and since he sang the best, it would be easier to sell him for a good price. Without longer hesitation, she reached in and firmly grasped him. Then without regarding the anxious twitter that came from the other members of the bird family, placed him in Oro's discarded cage, covered it with her shawl, and swiftly made her way down the stairs and into the street.

The few people who were astir at this early hour were hurrying too fast in an effort to keep warm to cast more than a passing glance at the woman in the faded shawl, and she made her way, without delay, through the empty streets to old Cicho's shop, where she seated herself on the stone step and settled down to wait until he should open the heavy door.

Nor was it long, for the old man, who slept in a room over the shop, at that moment chanced to be peering through the shutters, his nightcap still on his head.

"What can the woman want?" he muttered, rubbing his hands together. "She must have something to sell, for she never in the world would be on hand so early if it was to buy!"

In another moment he had turned the rusty key and, opening the big door, asked, with an ingratiating smile: "What can I do for you?"

He recognized her immediately. More than once he had wished he had not been so ready to dispose of *Il Canarino*; so fine a bird did not come his way often. Perhaps she wished him to buy him back. He hoped so.

After fumbling for a moment with her shawl, Margherita held out the cage and faltered:

"Perhaps you remember—my husband and I—and the little Rosa, bought a canary from you some months ago."

"*Si! Si!*" he answered, narrowing his eyes into a greedy slit and reaching out his hand for the cage. "What of it? Was he not all I represented?"

"*Ah, si!*" she answered, nervously clasping her hands. "That is not it. It is that my husband is sick, and we are poor. We must have money, or he will die! I have brought you Koto, one of *Il Canarino's* babies!"

"An untrained bird?" he murmured discontentedly. "An untrained bird! Because his father can sing does not mean that this one has a voice."

"But Pippa, his mother, comes of good stock!" she protested eagerly. "And he is not untrained. *Il Canarino* has given him lessons so that he can sing almost as well as can his father himself!"

At this point, Koto, delighted at being in the light, uttered a few joyous notes.

"Hmm!" The dealer shrugged his shoulders in an effort to conceal the delight he felt at a chance to get possession of what he now knew would prove a fine singer. "Hmm! It is a lottery. How much do you expect for him?"

Thus appealed to, Margherita knew not what to say. She hesitated.

"*Trenta lire!*"

"Impossible! What are you thinking of?" He threw up his hands in horror.

"Twenty—even fifteen?"

He shook his head. "His father I sold to you for only fifteen. How can you expect so much for so young a bird? *Venite!*" He lowered his voice. "On you I have compassion, and because your husband is sick, I will give you twelve lire."

She could have hugged him for joy as she mentally calculated how much she could buy for twelve lire. It was more than she had expected, and she did not know that he was congratulating himself on having so easily satisfied her.

Grudgingly he counted out the money, saying, "There,

.ake it!" and in response to her murmured "*Grazie*," he exclaimed grandly, "I have done well by you, my woman. If there are other birds to sell, bring them also to me! I am not one to cheat the poor!"

Drawing her shawl closer about her shoulders, she hurried along the streets, now filled with a busy throng. First, she would go to buy the medicine, for the last bottle had been empty for nearly a week, then to the market where she would get a nice fat hen that the sick man would relish. There, too, was the generous old woman who would sometimes slip in an extra stick of charcoal. Her spirits rose. Before the twelve lire were gone, surely Alessandro would be better.

For the first time in days, a faint smile was on her lips. In the meantime, Cicho had hung the little Koto where a streak of sunshine shone full upon his cage, and as the bird sang blithely, he slapped his sides, exclaiming, "*Bello canarino!* You'll do, you'll do!"

# 11

## Prosperity

Whether it was the good chicken broth, the medicine, or the warmer fire, I cannot say, but when the doctor came next, he pronounced the crisis past and the patient better.

Though Pip and Chita were both sold to old Cicho, Rosa did not complain, for was not her father improving and happiness once more coming to the home?

Spring breaks early in Italy, and by the time the first warm breezes blew, Alessandro was up and around. After that, he gained steadily. And it was a gala day when he donned his workman's blouse and went back to the factory.

In a few months, he was as strong as ever. And when he was given a much more important place the next year, and a substantial increase in wages, Margherita felt her cup was full to overflowing.

"It was all because Oro came to the rescue," she would say. "If he hadn't given that drowsy little chirp, I might never have thought of selling his babies." And with that, she would smooth the golden feathers and look affectionately into the beady eyes.

The sun of prosperity continued to shine upon the little family. They removed from the shabby rooms in the squalid district to larger and more pretentious quarters on the street of Santa Lucia.

Then how happy Rosa was! She had a room and a balcony all to herself, and an extended view over the bay to the beautiful islands of Capri and Ischia.

In this new home there was a best room, with a niche for a shrine, and great was the joy when Alessandro placed a statuette of the Virgin there. It was nearly three feet high, and when one stopped before it to cross oneself or murmur an *Ave Maria*, the sympathetic lips seemed to move in blessing.

In the wall below the shrine, Alessandro made a secret drawer where the purse filled with Rosa's gold pieces was kept, as well as his store of savings, which increased daily with the passing months.

Rosa was now a girl of fourteen. Her hair was as black as night and her complexion, a clear olive. When she laughed, she showed teeth like pearls. And her dark eyes snapped as she talked. She could dance the Tarantella as well as could her mother, and shake the tambourine with the same abandon.

Already a stalwart youth, Jacopo, by name, was casting admiring glances in her direction and had more than once walked by her side when the family went to the Park by the Bay and listened to the cheerful music of the band.

Beppo had grown into a strong little fellow and had begun to find a use for his sturdy arms and legs. What a voice he had! And what a temper! If things did not go his way, he would scream and cry until Margherita, distracted, would stand him to face the wall.

As for the birds, Oro was as ever adored by every member of the family. He had sympathized with them in sorrow and now rejoiced with them in their prosperity. Not but what he had had his troubles, and the whole family mourned with him the loss of faithful little Pippa.

Shortly before they had moved from the old quarters, she had sickened and died. Margherita, noticing that she drooped, had put an iron nail in the drinking water, hoping it would act as a tonic. But before long, the bird showed signs of asthma, and one morning they found her stiff and cold on the floor of the cage, with Oro uttering piteous little chirps.

It was plain he grieved over her loss, and not a member of the household had the heart even to suggest that her place be filled.

When first they moved to the new home, he seemed greatly puzzled and flew aimlessly about as if he missed his familiar haunts. But when he discovered the old clock ticking familiarly, he was quite content, preening his feathers and cocking his head as blithely as ever before the fine new looking glass in its ornate gilt frame.

Altogether, the whole family adapted themselves to the changed circumstances and settled down to enjoy life, when in the distance boomed the first guns that ushered in the World War.

# 12

## Marching Feet

*"In that August of all men's fate, Italy heard the blast of trumpets from across the Alps."*[1]

At first, it seemed a long way off—too far away for her to be greatly concerned. A quarrel between Germany and France. Let them settle it as they would. But Austria was a dangerous neighbor and an old enemy. The Italians had not forgotten the years when Venice was under her feet, and it was an open secret that, even now, she cast covetous eyes upon the beautiful city and openly exulted in the territory still in her possession. It was inevitable that, ere many months, Italy should be drawn into the struggle.

And so it was that in less than a year, the government declared war on Austria-Hungary. Even then, the people in general were not greatly aroused until there came rumors of an Austrian offensive. Then the peninsula was shaken from north to south, and through its length and breadth ran the tremor of war. On every side was heard the cry:

"Protect the frontier! Recover the lost territory! Chase the old hen out of Italy! *Viva il re! Viva l'Italia!*"[2]

---

1  *from "Scenes From Italy's War" by George Macaulay Trevelyan*
2  *Long live the king! Long live Italy!*

Victor Emmanuel is a favorite with his people. He is a conscientious, thoughtful man, incapable of any motive save for the interest and honor of his country. It is a common saying: "We have taken our king from the rough, energetic, soldierly family, neither dilettante, artistic, nor intellectual. He is a MAN!"

In this crisis, he was, as ever, their guide and leader, even a dictator in the Roman sense of the word.

He seemed omnipresent, counseling wisely and calling upon all to give their service to their country. His touring car was as familiar a sight in the camp of the army as it was on the streets of Rome.

Men hastened to enlist from Brindisi and surrounding towns; even from Sicily they poured.

Every village was bright with banners as motley hordes rallied, armed with revolvers, clubs, and canes, singing the songs of youth and giving the battle cries of ancient Rome.

Margherita never forgot the day when Alessandro came home in great excitement, exclaiming, "*Ē vero!* I go to fight for my country! There, there! Don't cry, *mia donna!*"[3] He stroked her hair as tenderly as he was wont to do in the old days when they were sweethearts at Capri. "Don't cry! We'll turn it into a glorious victory and get back all we ever lost. It won't be long before our men will cross the river!"

After dinner, when she was quieter and Rosa had gone to see the *Pulcinello*,[4] Alessandro took from the secret drawer the stout canvas bag which held his savings.

"See, my Margherita, how it bulges! There will be plenty to buy food for you and the little ones until I come back! No need to touch Rosa's money. And when the war is over, I am willing

---

3     *my wife*
4     Puppet show

to wager she will need the gold pieces. Jacopo is a lover to be proud of, and by that time, they will both be old enough!"

"*Si! Si!*" answered Margherita, entering into his mood. "They will make a lovely couple. We must give her as fine a wedding as any in all Naples."

And in talking of what they would do when he came back from the war, and in plans for future happiness, Margherita forgot to grieve.

But when the morning came and Alessandro had gone to the nearest recruiting office, the heartache came back.

She lived through the days that followed as if she were in a dream.

He was busy drilling, and all he thought of or talked about was war, war, war! Mechanically, she performed her daily tasks, but, though her eyes were dry, her heart was breaking. When, at last, he announced that his company would leave for the north that night, she could not speak but only clung to his hand while great, passionate sobs shook her frame.

But Rosa exclaimed how straight and handsome he looked in his uniform! And Beppo stretched out his arms in admiration to his father, whom, at first, he had not recognized. When Alessandro, like Hector in the old Homeric tale, lifted him into his arms, he was content and laughed aloud with glee.

At last Margherita dried her eyes and hung over him, bidding him to send her word as often as he could, and cautioning him to take every care that he might not fall ill, while Oro flew from his cage and perched upon his shoulder.

It was Rosa who spoke as she reached up and smoothed the fluttering little thing, "See, Oro wants to go with you!"

In an instant, Margherita grasped the idea. "And why should he not go? I have heard that soldiers often carry mascots, and that they protect from harm and bring them safely home."

"But you," her husband expostulated doubtfully, "what will you do without the little singing bird to keep you company?"

Without another word, she took the canary and, having placed it again in its cage, pressed it into his hand, urging: "I will have Rosa and the little Beppo. Do not refuse, for it will save me many a heartache if I know Oro is with you to cheer you with his song!"

He did no longer hesitate but held out his arm for a final embrace. Another instant and he was gone!

Gone, yet Margherita did not even then realize the bitter truth, not until hours after, when she sat by the window looking at the lights in the busy street. Suddenly she started—afar off there was the sound of the fife and the beating of the drum. They were coming. Alessandro had said they would pass down the Via Roma, and, afterwards, by way of the Santa Lucia. She went out on the balcony. Nearer came the music. They were playing Garibaldi's hymn:

"To arms!
Haste! Haste! Ye martial youth!"

And now the sound of marching feet! Nearer they came, accompanied by a cheering crowd. Nearer! She could distinctly see the forms of the men. Somewhere amid those marching hundreds setting out for the frontier was her husband.

She leaned over the balcony, tense in the effort to distinguish his form. There—they were passing! Now they had gone! She had not been able to recognize him.

Long she stood there, listening, until the sound of the marching feet grew fainter. At last she could not even hear the echoes of Garibaldi's words. Even the crowd dispersed.

Silently she crept to bed and lay there, thinking. Soon the street was quiet, save for the striking of a clock and the tramp of a policeman. But still she seemed to hear the sound of marching feet!

# 13

# THE MASCOT OF THE COMPANY

The soldiers' rendezvous was down by the Mole. It was a warm evening in April, and the sea breeze was most refreshing. Involuntarily, the men bared their heads, and a murmur ran through the gathering throngs: "*Il mare! Il mare!*"

Someone on the outskirts struck on his guitar the strains of "Dolce Napoli!", and instantly the song burst from strong men's throats:

"*O dolce Napoli
O suol beato!*"

Already the sun had set in a glory of crimson and gold, and the stars were beginning to twinkle. The streets, rising tier on tier from the shore, were ablaze with electricity, while far out on the bay, the lights in the war vessels and fishing boats were reflected in the rippling waters.

There is no city like Naples! Tears were in their eyes; some might never return.

There were many mascots, as Margherita had predicted. One man had a fat, squat, inarticulate turtle in his pocket, for which he evidently had inordinate affection. Another had a tiny kitten that kept poking its head out and uttering plaintive meows. A stocky fellow uncertainly balanced a globe of goldfish. There was more than one faithful dog; lizards were plentiful, and an owl with round, solemn eyes attracted a great deal of attention. All seemed to be more or less terrified by the confusion—only Oro was his own cheerful self, delighting in the lights, near and far, and from time to time singing his best, as if to hearten the company with his blithe notes.

Suddenly a voice called out: "The bird! The little singing bird! Let us make it the mascot of the company." Others, hearing, joined in the cry, gesticulating as only Neapolitans can. "*Urra! Urra!*[1] The little singing bird shall be our mascot!"

So it was that, as the ranks formed and marched through the lava-paved streets, Alessandro held high the cage so that all the company might see the bird that carried the responsibility for their welfare.

At the station, someone hummed, "*Addio, Mia Bella Napoli!*" and the chorus swelled as the soldiers crowded into the uncomfortable cars and gazed for the last time at the city so dear to them.

Slowly the late Italian train puffed its way toward the north. There were homesick hearts, yet the prevailing spirit was one of cheer. Many were the confidences and lasting friendships formed, for the Italian men are of quick impulses. There was much laughter and sport, much petting of mascots who, at times, became obstreperous and did their best to keep the atmosphere enlivened. And often, above the shrieks of the engine and the rumbling of the train, could be heard the notes of the little canary.

The company was detailed straight through to the frontier where the troops were holding positions along the Isonzo and pushing the stubborn offensive of 1916.

---

1   *Hooray! Hooray!*

# 14

## THE RED, WHITE, AND GREEN

The story of the war on the Italian frontier reads like a page from a romance. Nowhere were there greater acts of heroism: deeds that have gone down in history, bravery unparalleled in any other country.

There were miracles of road-making, and solid rock was hollowed out for the construction of tunnels and immense underground caverns.

There was a marvelous system of aerial airways, by which the mountains were looped, supplies conveyed to those guarding the tops, and the sick and wounded brought down the wires in cages.

There were massive rock summits excavated into labyrinthine fortresses, with stories of galleries, one above the other, grinning with cannon and machine guns.

For many weeks prior to the offensive, each night at sundown, by a wonderful feat of engineering, the water of the Isonzo was diverted, and in the shallow stream left in its bed, footbridges were built so as to be effectually concealed when the water flowed in its accustomed channel in the morning. It was planned to supplement these with pontoon bridges when the time of crossing should come.

It was a glorious country where the Italians were encamped that summer. On every side were fruit-laden hills, broken by the gorge of the blue, rushing Isonzo. At night, star-shells and rival searchlights revealed views of the scarred mountainsides and glimpses of distant plains.

For years, Gorizia had been a favorite health and pleasure resort of the Austrians. It was in a mild climate and overlooked by great towering mountains, now honeycombed with trenches rock-hewn by the genius of Italian engineers.

The brief messages Alessandro sent to Margherita were written in good spirits. He was well, she must not worry. It would not be long before the war would be over and the Austrians forever ousted from Italy. The general himself had taken a great fancy to Oro, insisting that the cage be hung above his desk, and often at night carried it into his rock chamber, that he might hear the cheery chirp the first thing in the morning. It was not an uncommon thing for the boys to borrow the canary in the chill evenings when they gathered about big, blazing fires; and as they talked about loved ones, the bird would fly from one to another, recalling cheerful rooms at home and scenes of peaceful farms and valleys far from the scene of the struggle. At times he was even carried to the front, where his glad song could be heard above the bursting bombs and the roar of cannon.

All Alessandro wrote was of great interest to Margherita and Rosa. Though they missed the little bird, it pleased them that he was doing his bit in helping to keep up the courage of those who were fighting for their king and country.

Through the summer things went well, and on the ninth of August, while the cannons fired from the rock fortifications and searchlights blinded the eyes of watching Austrians, the troops crossed the Isonzo, and the fair city of

Gorizia surrendered to the Italians.

Through the succeeding winter and summer, other victories followed. Farther and farther retreated the Austrians, and the red, white, and green waved on almost inaccessible summits.

Then Italy went wild with joy!

# 15

## A Dreary Christmas

Alessandro had been gone but a few days when Margherita made up her mind to move to less expensive quarters. Upon investigation, she learned there were rooms vacant in the building where they had previously lived.

"There's no knowing what may happen," she said, as she broached the subject to Rosa. "One can't be *sure* that the war will end this year, and with rents so high and food prices rising, we must save every possible *centesimo*. Besides, we don't need so large a place—" She stopped, choked with tears, and Rosa threw her arms about her while Beppo drew himself up proudly as if to say:

"Soon I'll be grown up and can make some money!"

It was true, they did not need so many rooms, but the old surroundings seemed shabbier than ever as they tried to make them homelike.

They worked with heavy hearts, missing the little canary more and more. The very goat looked dejected as it wearily climbed the stairs to give them milk. The good *caprajo* had gone to the war, and the boy who had taken his place was cruel and beat the patient animal.

Jacopo did all he could, and they came to depend greatly

upon him. At the least suggestion that the war might not end quickly, Rosa's heart would sink, for she knew it would not be long before he would arrive at the age for service. In fact, he was looking forward to the possibility and was regularly drilling with his companions.

In those days of anxiety, the statuette of the Virgin was a great comfort, and every night Margherita and Rosa told their beads before it and asked for her blessing on Alessandro and Oro so far away.

But their spirits were buoyed up by the good news that continued to filter through from the north. By nature optimistic, the Italians were confident that the war would soon be over, and their joy was unrestrained.

Then the tide turned!

As a bolt from the blue came the rumor that the Austrians had retaken Gorizia, and that the entire Italian front on the Isonzo had collapsed. A retreat had been ordered, and the victorious enemy were pursuing in hordes. Disaster was on every side. This was October 1917.

In despair, Margherita and Rosa clung to each other. The worst had come! It was Margherita who first roused and forced herself to think. With hostilities indefinitely prolonged, further effort must be made.

In spite of every economy, the bag that was so heavy when Allesandro left, was now pitifully light. The separation allowance was so small that they were unable to live on it. The rent, which had been increased for even these poor quarters, was now due. Food prices had soared to unbelievable heights. One of Rosa's gold pieces had already been spent, and it seemed as if the others would have to follow.

In the summer, fruit in northern Italy is abundant—

cherries, almonds, grapes, melons, and the *cava*, or delicious little black figs. One could almost live on figs alone, but winter was now approaching.

Then one morning, Margherita declared resolutely, "I will go to the macaroni factory and ask for work. You, my Rosa, must keep the house and look after Beppo!"

She had no difficulty in carrying out her purpose. Men were scarce, and the factory was running night and day to supply the enormous amount of macaroni required for the army as well as for the home consumption. The manager saw, at a glance, that Margherita was both strong and efficient.

The process of making macaroni is simple enough. After the flour has been thoroughly mixed with water, the dough is pressed into a thick paste and cut into cakes about a foot square and from one to three inches thick. These are placed in an iron cylinder, heated by steam, in the bottom of which is a copper plate perforated with holes. A cover, fitted to a great screw, is placed on top of the cylinder, and as the screw turns, the paste is slowly and steadily pressed through the openings, from which it comes in round hollow pipes which are afterwards cut into lengths of about three feet and spread on wire frames to dry.

The work and confinement, together with the constant worry, told on Margherita, and she grew steadily thinner and paler.

Rosa lost her youthful curves and looked old beyond her years. What with attention to the home and care of the active Beppo, to say nothing of the bandages which her nimble fingers made under the direction of the Red Cross, her time was filled to overflowing. All through October discouraging news continued to come. It was no wonder the morale of the army was almost gone; many had been away from their homes for over two years, and the third winter was coming on. Hundreds had perished from cholera and other diseases, to say nothing of those who had died in battle.

At heart, the Italian peasant is simple and intensely human. He is devoted to his home, and his sympathies are centered on his little farm and loved ones. Why should he not grumble? What had he to show for the years of hardship and struggle? All that had been gained was now lost. "*Andiamos à casa!*"[1] became the cry as hundreds deserted.

Then, suddenly, the word flashed through the length and breadth of the peninsula that the men would make a final effort at the Piave, if the people at home would stand back of them! All depended on that "IF."

Instantly, a wave of patriotism swept the country. Men and women repented their murmurings, their crying for peace when there was no peace, their discouraging letters to the soldiers at the front.

Those who, through infirmity, were not able to join the ranks, even the paralyzed and blind, did their part in rousing enthusiasm; the young and the old alike crowded to offer their services.

Rosa herself hung an amulet about Jacopo's neck and bade him go. "Even if," she faltered, as she clung to him, "even if you—never come back!"

So passed November. Margherita had not heard from Alessandro for months. Even with her wages from the factory, it was all they could do to keep from starving. There was not a *centesimo* in the stout bag, of whose weight her husband had been so proud, and all of Rosa's gold pieces were gone.

December came and Christmas, the greatest of all the

---

1    *Let's go home!*

*feste*[2], when the Neapolitan makes merry with bagpipe and flageolet, when the twang of the guitar and the rap-a-tap of the tambourine is heard on every side, when booths are set up in the streets and vendors cry insistently, "Buy! Buy!"

Ah! The cakes and sweets, the most delicious of confections to the Neapolitan palate!

Alas! This year, no Christmas fair was held; there were only a few scattered booths, looking decidedly out of place.

By government edict, there were no cakes or sweets. Sugar and flour must be conserved to feed the soldiers, so far away.

The American child dances about his Christmas tree, but the Neapolitans gather around the *presepe*, or manger, where, on the twenty-fourth, is laid the effigy of the Christ-child. Often is shown the grotto or stable, with the Virgin Mother proudly holding the Child, while behind stands Joseph, and in the background, the ox and the ass keep watch together.

Before the shrines, candles are reverently burned, and the Novena or Christmas hymn is sung in every home.

But this year all was different. There was no *presepe*. Little Beppo cried in vain for gifts. One tiny stick of charcoal flickered miserably, and a single candle was all Margherita felt she could afford to burn before the shrine.

Their hearts were full of thoughts of Alessandro, Jacopo, and Oro, and their voices trembled as they tried to be brave and sing the Christmas hymn.

---

[2]  *festivals*

# 16

## THE LITTLE GOLDEN FEATHER

To say that the brave stand made by Alessandro and his companions was due to the cheering notes of the little canary would be too much to claim. But it is a fact that, in the general panic and confusion, with many deserting, they remained true and loyal.

It seemed nothing short of the impossible for the struggling remnants of the Italian army to hold those mountain positions behind the Piave and force back the frantic Austrian hordes— only three miles more and the enemy would stand on top of the great wall of mountains; the Piave frontier would be gone and Venice lost.

The men had not even the protection of trenches, but lived in tents and holes in the limestone until huts could be constructed. But one thing never failed, the succulent meal of pasta, which, as by some miracle, was always served hot and appetizing. Was it Napoleon who made the assertion that men fight on their stomachs?

Their courage was almost superhuman. *"Non si passa"*[1] was the stubborn motto, as lads of seventeen and eighteen, sent up from the depots, saved their country again and again.

---

1  *"You cannot pass"*

Nor was Italy forgotten by the Allies. France, England, and America hastened to give every assistance in their power in this critical juncture.

From time to time, the king was with the soldiers, encouraging them by his presence and sharing their hardships. The feeling that existed between him and the troops was as strong as it had been two years before, when one Austrian town after another had surrendered, and six hundred children at the foot of Mt. Stol flung themselves before him, forming with their bodies the word "Italia!"

In these hours of discouragement, the cry was still, "*Viva l'Italia! Viva il re!*"

After a few weeks, the regiments were moved into huts constructed close under the edge of a certain cliff in which a cavern had been excavated, where the general had his headquarters. As usual, at night, Oro's cage hung above his cot.

It was his custom to surrender his room to Victor Emmanuel when at the front, and little did anyone suspect that, on this particular occasion, an Austrian spy had recognized the familiar Fiat car climbing the heights and was seeking an opportunity to make an attempt on the king's life. Concealed in a niche in the rocks, he had discovered where His Majesty would pass the night. When all was still and the sentry at the other end of his beat, he climbed stealthily up the cliff to where an aperture had been made in the rock wall, for the purpose of admitting fresh air into the chamber.

It was a perilous thing to do, and more than once his heart almost stopped beating as pieces of loose rock crumbled under his feet. But, at last, he gained the desired point, and holding his ear to the opening, heard only regular breathing.

In one hand he held a bomb, and, cautiously thrusting in his free hand, he felt for a ledge on which to leave it. Ah! He had found it, but to make sure, took his flashlight from his pocket. Again he held his ear close to the opening. All was still. Even if the orderly and King's Guard were in the anteroom, it was probable they would not see the tiny beam of light. He must run his chance of that. In another moment, he had flashed it.

What was that? A sleepy chirp. A cursed bird! Who would ever have thought of a canary in such a place? Swiftly thrusting in the other arm, he deposited the bomb, then turned to slink away just as Oro burst into joyous song, having mistaken the flash of light for a streak of dawn.

Having swung himself down, he ran for his life with a muttered, "Drat that bird!" just as the smoking bomb was discovered, and the whole camp burst into uproar. In an instant, a dozen or more men set off in hot pursuit, while the glad cry rent the air:

"The bird! The little singing bird has saved the king! *Urra! Urra!*"

Alessandro had been on the sick list for a few days and was convalescing in the field hospital. As the noise penetrated the sick wards, he stirred uneasily. What had happened?

Then a fellow sufferer reached over and touched his arm. "Man, do you hear? They say your bird has saved the king!"

At first he could not comprehend what it was the man meant. Then, as the cry came again and again through the open window, a look of great joy spread over his face, and he repeated over and over: "*Buone notizie!*[2] Oro has saved the king! How proud Margherita and Rosa will be when I tell

---

2      Good news!

them the *grande* news!"

Then—wonder of wonders! In a few moments, the king himself came in, saying, as he bent over his bed, "I want to see the man who owns the bird—the bird who saved my life!"

"*Si*, Your Majesty!" Alessandro faltered, almost dumb at the honor which had come to him, and listening breathlessly as the king went on: "What can I do to show my gratitude?"

"Oh, nothing! Nothing!" answered Alessandro, more overwhelmed than ever.

"But I must have the bird shown to my queen! We must have his song in the palace! Name your price!"

Alessandro was silent. How could he sell his bird? And yet, to refuse would be discourteous.

"Come, you cannot make it too high. I must have him!" the king repeated, a little impatiently.

"But, *signor!*" Alessandro stammered, "I cannot sell the bird. He belongs to my wife and Rosa. We have had him for years, and they would grieve if I did not bring him home! Your Majesty, pray forgive!" And he caught the king's hand imploringly.

"*Capisco!*"[3] The king's expression softened. "I understand, my man. Keep your bird; at least, I may take to my queen this little feather which I found upon the floor."

At sight of the feather, the tears came to the sick man's eyes. He rose on his elbow and answered passionately, "*Grazie! Grazie!* I will tell my wife and Rosa and the little Beppo of the generosity of the king!"

"Nay, nay, my man," was the response. "I would have paid you well, but since you would not have it so, when the war is over, bear this message to your wife and children: 'The King does not forget!'" Then, with a kindly expressed wish for his

---

3   *I understand!*

speedy recovery, Victor Emmanuel was gone.

All day Alessandro lay in a kind of stupor. It seemed as if he must have dreamed the incident. Yet, over and over again floated through the window:

"The bird! The little singing bird has saved the king! Long live the king!"

# 17

## The Homecoming

Everyone knows the story of the rout: how, in June, the last great offensive was launched; how the Austrian infantry even crossed the Piave but was forced, after eight days, to withdraw under cover of darkness, and Italy was saved!

We are told that the whole army shouted and sang beneath the stars because the war was over and the invader driven from their country.

Soon they were on their way home—the sick and the wounded, the war-torn and weary. "*Andiamos a casa*" was heard on every side, but this time it was a cry of triumph, not the despairing plaint of vanquished troops.

Home! Home! Back to the slopes of sunny Italy. Back to their little farms! To their vineyards! To their fishermen's nets! Back, it might be, to shabby rooms and squalid side streets. What mattered? They were going HOME—to sweethearts and families!

And all along the way, they were fairly worshiped by people mad with joy. In Venice, the spirit of the old Carnival days prevailed. At Padua, crowds gathered about the statue of Garibaldi the Liberator. It seemed as if he were alive and watching—that graven image, hand on sword belt, seemed to watch and know as the company of men filed past, and one of the generals set between his arms the staff of the flag he loved.

On and on they marched, and everywhere met cheering throngs; men and women waving flags and banners, bearing in their hands *thyrsi* or peeled fir saplings, and wearing on their heads garlands of leaves, the symbols of victory.

The horses were decorated with ribbons and feathers, while the donkeys, bright with tassels, tinkled little bells as they walked.

It was a perfect pandemonium of sound: dogs yelping, donkeys braying, and people shouting amid the fanfare of trumpets and the beating of drums.

On, on they marched through beautiful rolling country, with its splendor of fruit trees and vineyards, and from every throat went up the cry, "Long live the king! *Viva l'Italia!*"

In Florence and Rome, the demonstrations, while quite orderly, were equally hilarious, and then those who were left boarded the trains for the south. They were tired, these soldiers who had borne so much, and nearly all dozed in spite of efforts to keep awake. But as they neared Naples, and one or two caught glimpses of the shining waters of the bay, a cry went up: "*Il mare! Il mare!*" And in another moment, from all throats burst the song:

"*O dolce Napoli,
O suol beato!*"

It was late when the slow Italian train puffed into the station. They had been so delayed that few were there to meet them or knew when to expect them.

They broke ranks down by the Mole—some to go on to Capri, Sorrento, and surrounding towns; others to Brindisi, and thence to Sicily.

They were almost exhausted. Yet, before they separated, one last "*Urra!*" was given for Oro, their mascot, who had brought them safely home.

Thin and worn from the hardships of the two and a half years he had been away, Alessandro, cage in hand, threaded the dirty side street, climbed the dark stairs, and turned the handle of the door.

In an instant, Margherita, who was lying wide-eyed and tense on the couch, was in his arms. Soon Rosa and Beppo, wakened by the commotion, were there too, and tears of happiness streamed from his eyes as he held them close and tried to tell, all in one minute, the experiences to which it would require months to do justice.

When they turned to lavish praise upon the little canary, they found him too busy enjoying the hemp seed they had provided as a special treat to even notice them. After which, he took a full fifteen minutes to preen his bedraggled feathers, then drooped his weary head and, more sensible than they, was soon fast asleep.

# 18

## THE MARRIAGE FEAST

Jacopo did not arrive until a day or two later, having been detained in the hospital until he had recovered from his wounds. He had lost his left arm but proudly wore on his breast the *croce al merito* (the Italian cross of honor).

You may take my word that there was no happier sweetheart in all Naples than was Rosa as he clasped her to his heart. One could see at a glance that he was finer than ever. And when he declared they must be married at once, she was all smiles. Suddenly, her face changed. She remembered that she had no dowry now that the gold pieces had been spent, but when she falteringly mentioned this to him, he only laughed and answered, "I have but one arm, but what difference does it make? Look you!" And he stretched it out that she might see how strong and muscular it was. "Do you not think I can make as good a living with the one I have left as many can make with both?"

He laughed again, and she hid her blushing face against his shoulder, while Margherita, in the kitchen, unfolded to Alessandro her plans for the wedding and the feast that should follow.

"We will bid the neighbors and friends," she said, "for all

will wish to take our Rosa by the hand, not to mention their curiosity to look upon the brave canary who did his bit for Italy at the front. Yes," she went on musingly, "we'll have music and feasting, for the war is over, and it is well that we should rejoice."

When Alessandro reminded her that there was little money to spend, she only laughed and answered, as good wives have done since the world began, "Leave that to me," and went on with her preparations.

When the guests were bidden, there was no one forgotten. There were relatives and immediate friends of the happy pair, as well as those who had fought by Jacopo's and Alessandro's sides. There were Margherita's companions in the macaroni factory, the proprietor himself not disdaining to accept their hospitality and bearing with him a goodwill offering of an enormous box of pasta. Even the *caprajo* was remembered, and old Cicho, who managed to climb the stairs in spite of his rheumaticky limbs.

All were in holiday attire: many of the *contadine*[1] in beribboned dresses and becrinolined skirts that had done duty for a half century or more; others in bright bodices, with simple crossed kerchiefs; while certain dandies among the men were resplendent in short jackets, blue, green, or brown, with light waistcoats and, perchance, sky-blue trousers.

Altogether it was a gala company, and it was hard, indeed, to imagine a bonnier bride than Rosa, attired in Margherita's own wedding petticoat, trimmed with rich lace and heavily embroidered.

She wore a black velvet bodice with a yellow scarf wound about her waist; large gold hoops dangled bewitchingly from her ears, and a brooch of coral held her kerchief.

---

1    peasants

They were a merry, carefree gathering, and attention was about equally divided between the happy couple and the little bird whose song had saved the king and who seemed the very spirit of joyousness on this festive occasion.

As for the feast, words fail to do justice to its excellence. First and foremost, there was the capitone eel, always a delicacy, and for this festive occasion, Margherita had spared no pains to make it especially appetizing, so profusely was it anointed with olive oil and so piquantly was it seasoned with garlic, anchovy, cheese, and bacon.

Besides the eel, there were both snails and oysters, with a goodly supply of spaghetti and salad. Now that the war was over and the ban had been lifted from sweets, the cakes and dolces were rich, indeed, especially suited to every palate.

After the feast was over, the musicians took their places, and soon was heard the sound of the fife and bagpipe. There was even a wheezy old hand-organ, as well as the inevitable Jew's harp, while above all other sounds could be heard the notes of the little canary, singing as if his throat would burst. It was not long before, led by Rosa and Jacopo, many joined in the Tarantella. Suddenly, amid the general pandemonium and the rap-a-tap of the tambourine, there came a knock at the door. And a moment later, who should step into the room but Victor Emmanuel!

# 19

## THE KING DOES NOT FORGET

He was in uniform, with medals and insignia about his neck and on his breast. He hesitated on the threshold, and every person of the whole assemblage felt the kindliness in his eyes, the true democracy of his bearing.

As the music ceased suddenly, he came forward and, advancing to Alessandro, quietly addressed him.

"I do not wish to intrude upon this happy scene, nor will I claim your attention but a moment."

With that, his piercing eyes lighted upon Oro swinging in his cage, and with the simplest of gestures, he went on:

"The king does not forget, and I have come to express, in some slight measure, my appreciation of what the little singing bird once did for me."

Thrusting his hand into his pocket, he drew out a gold box, the cover of which was stamped with the royal crest, interwoven with a gold feather. Handing this to Alessandro, he continued.

"This is for your daughter, to whom you say the bird belongs and whose wedding day this is. It is my wish that she should accept it, and, in making use of the money it contains, remember that each golden florin carries with it the king's gratitude."

Before the astonished Alessandro could falter a grateful, "*Grazie*, Your Majesty!" the king was gone.

Margherita was the first to recover. And snatching the box from her husband's hand, held it up that all might see, then quickly bore it away and hid it in a safe place, murmuring to herself as she did so, "It is best to be careful. They are all honest enough, without doubt, but—one—never—knows."

In the general buzz that followed the amazing incident, perhaps the comment made by old Cicho was most characteristic:

"To think I sold that bird for only fifteen lire!" And at once he registered a vow that the price of all his canaries should straightway advance.

After the guests had gone, Alessandro and Margherita, Jacopo and Rosa, gathered about the table, still piled with the remains of the feast, and counted the gold pieces.

There were fully twice as many as the good priest had brought on that other memorable occasion, and each one was worth nearly ten dollars.

It was a sum in arithmetic that was fairly staggering. And when Jacopo announced that they amounted to what, in American money, would be fully two hundred and fifty dollars, they were appalled by the undreamed wealth. What would they do with it all? Had ever a bride so rich a dowry?

At last Rosa spoke, smiling radiantly as she tapped Jacopo on the shoulder. "We will buy a home in Capri. What say you? Would it not be to your liking?"

"Even so!" And he hugged his bride to his heart with delight. "And the mother and father and the lad, Beppo, shall share it with us!"

At the words, tears streamed down Margherita's cheeks,

and Alessandro's voice was husky as he wiped his eyes with his handkerchief.

To them both, nothing could be so absolutely wonderful as to spend their declining years in Capri.

# 20

## Happiness

A little back from a winding road that zigzags down the sunny hillside is the island home of Rosa and Jacopo. It is not unlike other houses in Capri, in that it is a one-story adobe and pink in color.

Over it clambers a gnarled old grapevine whose leaves provide shelter from the scorching rays of the midday sun. In the season, great bunches of purpling fruit festoon the windows. In front of the house are other grapevines and a few olive trees, while behind are a neat pigsty and a full acre of land.

In the doorway hangs Oro's cage—he is as blithe as ever, this little canary, his feathers as yellow, his beady eyes as keen. He loves to swing lazily back and forth, or better still, fly out in the fresh, clear air.

Five years have passed—five happy years. Three sturdy children have been born to Rosa and Jacopo. The twins—Manuel and Victoria—named for the king, are three years old; while Rosita, the *bambina* is just four months, with hair and eyes, even now, as black as her mother's.

Jacopo is a fisherman, and one may see him any day down by the bay, in Phrygian cap and drawers and jacket of a coarse cloth. At his side works Beppo, a fine, stocky fellow. It will not be long before he will begin to cast sheep's eyes at the pretty fisher maidens, or perchance seek to attract the attention of some barelegged donkey girl, with Grecian profile, as she steers a stubborn quadruped by the tail.

Margherita, practical as ever, finds her time well occupied in the household, while Alessandro tills the acre of ground or sits in absolute contentment in the shade of a great vine or silvery olive, where he peacefully smokes his pipe and thinks of the stirring days of the past.

Often he takes his grandchildren on his knees and tells them tales of life at the front. They never tire of listening, although much he says is still beyond their comprehension. But the stories they love most to hear are of the little canary, and with awed fingers, they touch the treasured relics—the tiny cross and the feather on the golden box.

They sit with rapt attention as he tells how Oro won the bit of ribbon at the exhibition, how happy he was with his little mate, and how the sacrifice of Pippa's babies was the means of again bringing health and happiness to the home.

At this point, Alessandro always stops to clear his voice and then goes on dramatically: "He was the mascot of the company, our brave canary! It was his song that heartened the homesick men and gave them courage. As for the king! That dastardly rascal would have killed him but for our little singing bird!"

At this juncture, Manuel and Victoria almost fall off their grandfather's knees in sheer excitement as they echo in their childish voices:

"It was our little singing bird who saved the king."
"*Urra! Urra!*"

Even Rosita seems to understand, and laughs aloud in glee

as she points her fat forefinger to the dainty feathered thing that flits among the branches or lights upon her baby head, singing, rolling, trilling in ecstasy.

*Such a little thing! Such a dainty little thing!*
*All made up of trills and tremolos:*
*And yet so brave of heart!*

The End

# More Books from The Good and the Beautiful Library!

*Trini, The Strawberry Girl*
by Johanna Spyri

*Black Hawk*
by Arthur J. Beckhard

*The Scarlet Oak*
by Cornelia Meigs

*The Touch of Magic*
by Lorena A. Hickok

www.thegoodandthebeautiful.com